The Trip

Kasia Reay

Illustrated by Tika and Tata

Schofield & Sims

It was a br<u>igh</u>t m<u>or</u>n<u>ing</u> and Flu<u>ff</u> the rabbit had a plan. "Let's go on a trip to the c<u>oa</u>st," she said.

It was <u>too</u> <u>far</u> to hop, so the rabbits went to <u>look</u> f<u>or</u> a lift.

Can we j<u>oi</u>n you dogs in the tru<u>ck</u>?

"<u>Th</u>r<u>ee</u> of you can. Jump in," said the dogs.

So <u>three</u> rabbits got into the tru<u>ck</u>.
But it was hot in the cab and dogs
b<u>ar</u>k a lot!

Can we j<u>oi</u>n you c<u>ow</u>s on the tram?

"<u>Three</u> of you can. Jump on," said the c<u>ow</u>s.

So <u>thr<u>ee</u></u> rabbits got onto the tram. But they got stu<u>ck</u> in a <u>corner</u> and <u>cows</u> m<u>oo</u> a lot!

"Three of you can. Jump on," said the pigs.

So <u>thr</u><u>ee</u> rabbits got onto the tr<u>ai</u>n. But it was a t<u>igh</u>t fit and pigs sn<u>or</u>t a lot!

So just Fluff was left. She began to hop along in the fresh air.

She did not stop at... the ro<u>ck</u>s on the r<u>ai</u>ls... <u>or</u> the tr<u>ee</u> on the r<u>oa</u>d... <u>or</u> the <u>sh</u><u>ee</u>p on the tra<u>ck</u>.

Hop, hop, hop... to the c<u>oa</u>st!

After reading

Comprehension questions

1 Look at page 2. How many rabbits can you count?

2 Look at page 2. What is Fluff the rabbit's plan?

3 Look at page 3. Why do the rabbits decide not to hop to the coast? What do they plan to do instead?

4 Look at page 5. Why were the rabbits uncomfortable sitting with the dogs in the truck?

5 Look at page 12. Do you think the other rabbits will make it to the coast to join Fluff the rabbit?

Answers

1 Ten.

2 Fluff's plan is to go on a trip to the coast with her rabbit friends.

3 It is too far for them to hop to the coast, so they will get a lift instead.

4 It was hot and noisy with the dogs barking in the truck.

5 Your child may give a range of responses. For example: *I don't think the other rabbits will make it to the coast because rocks/a tree/sheep blocked their journeys. I think that the other rabbits will copy Fluff and hop the rest of the way to the coast.* Encourage your child to explain their ideas.

Published by **Schofield & Sims Ltd**
7 Mariner Court, Wakefield, West Yorkshire WF4 3FL, UK
Telephone 01484 607080
www.schofieldandsims.co.uk

This edition copyright © Schofield & Sims Ltd, 2021
First published in 2021

Author: **Kasia Reay**
Kasia Reay has asserted her moral rights under the Copyright, Designs and Patents Act, 1988, to be identified as the author of this work.

Illustrator: **Tika and Tata**

Based on an original idea by Kasia Reay and Selina Rayner.

British Library Cataloguing in Publication Data
A catalogue record for this book is available from the British Library.

Design by **Ledgard Jepson Ltd**
Printed in the UK by **Page Bros (Norwich) Ltd**

ISBN 978 07217 1693 0

My Letters and Sounds

Structured daily phonics teaching aligned with *Letters and Sounds*

The Trip

Fluff and her friends want to go to the coast. But how will they get there?

More books in Phase Four:

Phase Four

Yellow Band

Fiction

Phonics focus:
CVCC words and CCVC words

Tricky words:
said, so

ISBN 978 07217 1693 0   **£3.95** (retail price)

ISBN 978-07217-1693-0

9 780721 716930

MIX
Paper from responsible sources
FSC® C023114

Schofield&Sims

www.schofieldandsims.co.uk